FISHING
FOR
METHUSELAH

ROGER ROTH

HARPERCOLLINSPUBLISHERS

With love and gratitude to my wonderful wife,
Darlene "Lulu" Friedman,
who—though it pains me deeply to admit it—
came up with some of the best lines in the book

Fishing for Methuselah   Copyright © 1998 by Roger Roth   Printed in the U.S.A.   All rights reserved.

Library of Congress Cataloging-in-Publication Data
Roth, Roger.
Fishing for Methuselah / Roger Roth.
p.   cm.
Summary: After having competed with each other in everything and been outwitted by Methuselah,
best friends Ivan and Olaf finally find something on which they can cooperate.
ISBN 0-06-027592-8
[1. Best friends—Fiction.   2. Competition (Psychology)—Fiction.
3. Cooperativeness—Fiction.   4. Fishing—Fiction.]   I. Title.
PZ7.R736Fi 1998   97-49666
[E]—dc21   CIP
AC

Typography by Alicia Mikles
1   2   3   4   5   6   7   8   9   10
❖
First Edition
Visit us on the World Wide Web!
http://www.harperchildrens.com

Ivan and Olaf were best friends.

These two fellows, who lived way up in the North Country, had been best friends since they were no bigger than bear cubs. But to see them carrying on, you might not think they were friends at all. In fact, you might wonder if they even *liked* each other!

It didn't matter if it was paddling canoes, climbing trees, or snowshoeing up a mountainside, one was always trying to outdo the other.

When Ivan ate thirty flapjacks for breakfast one morning, Olaf devoured thirty-*five* with a side order of bacon and home fries. Then he grinned and said to the waitress, "Could I see the dessert menu, *please!*"

Then there was the time Olaf grabbed his ax and, in one hour, split and stacked a pile of firewood ten feet high. Ivan turned right around and split and stacked a pile fifteen feet high in the same amount of time. Then he inspected his ax closely and said, "Gee, Olaf, I need to sharpen this blade. It's *really* slowin' me down!"

Ivan and Olaf never agreed on much, either. If Ivan said, "I think we're gonna have a beautiful day today!" Olaf muttered, "Looks like snow to me."

You get the idea.

Every morning Ivan and Olaf would meet at Lulu's North Country Diner for breakfast and a quick arm wrestling match before they went off to work. And every morning Lulu and her customers would be forced to listen to that day's argument.

This squabbling always reached its peak right before the Winter Carnival up at Moosehead Lake. People came from miles around to eat home cooking and hear a real live polka band. There were all sorts of great contests, too—dogsled races, bobsled runs, snowshoe dancing, and barrel jumping. The most popular events were the ice fishing competition and the grand finale—the Fabulous Ice Sculpture Contest.

Of course, Ivan and Olaf would compete in just about every carnival event, but it was the ice fishing contest that really got them stirred up. Ivan and Olaf weren't satisfied with trying to catch the largest fish and winning first prize in the competition. They had themselves a private bet on which of them would catch the biggest fish in all of Moosehead Lake—the famed fish Methuselah.

"Hey, Ivan!" Olaf grinned. "Methuselah is mine this year. You better get your five bucks ready."

"That's a laugh," Ivan retorted. "I can smell that fish cookin' on my stove right now!"

"Ah, why don't you guys give it a rest?" said Lulu, rolling her eyes. "I've been fishin' that lake for twenty years. I've never even seen Methuselah. You'll never catch him. He's just too darn smart."

"Make no mistake about it," Olaf boomed. "*I* will catch Methuselah!"

"No, *I* will!" boasted Ivan.

Methuselah was the oldest, the largest, and by far the craftiest fish in all of Moosehead Lake. At least that's what the local fishermen said. Everybody knew somebody who knew someone who had almost caught Methuselah. But the big fish always got away.

Some said Methuselah was a fat green beast with great shiny teeth. Others said he was long, thin, and slithery, with giant shifty eyes. Still others said there was no such fish at all—it was just fishermen telling tales, as they're known to do now and then.

Ivan and Olaf met at daybreak on the morning of the ice fishing contest. They gathered up their gear, a toboggan, some food, and their dogs—Tarzan and Daisy—and headed out for Moosehead Lake.

"I hope you brought your money," Olaf said as he climbed into the truck. "'Cause I'm catchin' that big fish today."

"Keep dreamin', my friend," Ivan retorted. "It's *my* hook Methuselah waits for!"

When the two men arrived at the lake, the icy expanse was already dotted with fishermen hoping to catch that year's prize fish. Ivan and Olaf loaded their gear on the toboggan and trudged out onto the ice. The wind howled and the ice creaked as Ivan and Olaf slowly made their way farther and farther out on the vast lake—leaving all the other fishermen far behind.

At last Ivan came to a halt. "*This* is where Methuselah awaits me!"

Ivan grabbed his auger and began to drill.

"Hah! You'll find no fish there," scoffed Olaf as he swaggered past. "It's out *here* Methuselah lingers, my foolish friend."

Then Olaf started to drill. Seeing this, Ivan snatched up his drill and marched past Olaf.

Olaf shook his head and scratched his whiskers. Not to be outdone, he grabbed his drill once more and stomped past Ivan.

Before they knew it, Ivan and Olaf had wandered farther than anyone had gone before. Going that far from shore was considered much too dangerous. The ice was very thin, and some patches of the lake weren't frozen over at all!

It was there, on the thinnest ice on the lake, that Ivan and Olaf each drilled their holes. The men slipped minnows onto their hooks and plunked them down into the cold, dark water.

There was nothing to do now but wait.

Ivan and Olaf sat silently staring into their fishing holes.

"Bah!" Olaf snarled to himself. "That Ivan drives me nuts. He took the spot I wanted. Now he'll be the one to catch Methuselah!"

Blowing his nose loudly, Ivan thought, "Blast it all! I won't catch anything but a cold fishing in this stupid spot. I should be where Olaf is. Now he's gonna catch the big fish, win the contest, and take my five dollars!"

The longer they sat there, the angrier the two men became.

To get his mind off his troubles, Olaf began to whistle.

"Olaf!" growled Ivan. "Stop that noise. You're scarin' away the fish."

"Ha!" Olaf scoffed. "You blew your nose so loud, you probably already scared away every fish in the lake. Besides, you took my fishing spot!"

Ivan blew his nose even louder as he stood up and faced Olaf. "I took *your* spot? You took *my* spot!"

"Says who?" shouted Olaf.

"Says me!" yelled Ivan.

The two men stood glaring at each other.

Meanwhile, down below the ice, Methuselah was listening.

Now, there's a little-known fact about fish. They hate bickering. And Methuselah was no exception. For years he'd been listening to these two knuckleheads wrangling with each other. And they were truly getting on his nerves.

Just then, Methuselah heard Ivan yell to Olaf, "Ah, keep your lousy spot! You couldn't catch that big dumb fish if it jumped out and kissed ya!"

That did it. It was time these two fools learned a lesson.

Methuselah signaled Ivan's and Olaf's minnows to swim circles around each other until the two fishing lines were tangled into a large, strong knot. After setting the frightened minnows free, the great fish grabbed hold of the lines and began to pull.

"Whoa!" yelled Ivan as he felt a tremendous tug on his line. "I've got him, Olaf! I've got Methuselah!"

But Olaf felt a great tug on his line, too. "Oh no, you don't. I've got Methuselah on *my* line!"

The two men pulled on their fishing poles with all their might. C-C-C-C-CRACK!

Ivan and Olaf felt the ice tremble beneath their feet. Tarzan and Daisy yelped.

"What was that?" Olaf gulped.

"I-I-I don't know," Ivan sputtered. "Look there!"

The two men squinted into the howling wind.

"Water! It's open water!" Olaf cried. "We've busted loose and we're drifting away from shore!"

"Oh, we're goners now!" Ivan moaned. "And it's all your fault. You *had* to fish way out here, didn't you?"

"My fault? It's *your* fault!" snapped Olaf. "You're the one who said this is where Methuselah was."

As Ivan, Olaf, and their dogs drifted farther away on their tiny island of ice, the men looked around frantically, trying to figure a way out of their fix.

"I know!" Ivan exclaimed. "Maybe we can use the toboggan as a raft."

"Maybe if I tie these buckets to the sides, it might float," Olaf said.

"Good idea!" Ivan added, "I'll try to rig up some paddles."

The fishermen quickly set to work. In just a few minutes they had fashioned themselves a raft and two makeshift paddles.

"Well, here goes nothin'," Ivan said as they pushed the toboggan onto open water.

Ivan, Olaf, Tarzan, and Daisy carefully climbed aboard.

"She floats!" Ivan cheered.

The two men paddled and paddled with all their strength, but the wind was against them and the shoreline got no closer.

"It's no use!" cried Ivan. "We'll never make it."

"We've got to keep goin'," panted Olaf. "It's our only hope!"

On and on they battled the waves, but the raft seemed to be standing still.

Methuselah watched the raft thrash about. The big fish hated bickering, but he wasn't heartless. He decided to take pity on the hapless fishermen and their dogs.

Suddenly a great *thump* shook the raft. Tarzan and Daisy jumped up, howling.

"Stay still!" yelled Ivan. "You'll tip us over!"

"Look! We're moving!" exclaimed Olaf, pointing toward shore. Sure enough, the raft gathered speed as it headed toward the shoreline and solid ice.

"Watch out!" yelled Olaf. "Get ready to hit!"

Bam . . . Splash . . . Whoosh crashed the toboggan, throwing Ivan, Olaf, Tarzan, and Daisy head over heels. Olaf and Ivan lay dazed on the ice.

Hearing a thunderous *slap*, the men lifted their heads just as a huge green shadowy form plunged beneath the water and ice.

"Did you see that?" Ivan asked.

"Yeah!" Olaf said, rubbing his eyes. "I mean, I think so!"

Ivan and Olaf got up slowly and dusted snow off themselves. They walked back across the frozen lake in silence.

On the drive back to town, Olaf was the first to speak.

"I'm glad you thought of using that toboggan for a raft, Ivan. I guess you really saved our necks!"

"It wouldn't have worked," Ivan replied humbly, "if you hadn't thought of using the buckets for floats."

The next morning Ivan and Olaf met at Lulu's North Country
Diner for breakfast, as usual.

"Hey, boys!" Lulu greeted them. "How was the ice fishing contest?
Catch that old Methuselah this year?"

The two men glanced sideways at each other.

"Naw," said Ivan, shaking his head. "Nobody's ever gonna catch
that big fish."

"You boys sure have changed your tune," Lulu said in disbelief.

"You were right, Lulu. That fish is just too darn smart," Olaf added,
winking at Ivan.

After three helpings of flapjacks, bacon, home fries, and eggs—and,
of course, a quick arm wrestling match—Ivan and Olaf got up to pay
their check. They didn't want to be late for the last day of the Winter
Carnival.

"Hey, fellas," Lulu said. "See you at the ice sculpture contest?"

"I'll be there," declared Olaf.

"And *I'll* be there," added Ivan. "Winnin' first prize, too."

Lulu shook her head and smiled as the two men hurried out the door. "Those boys will never change," she laughed to herself.

But Lulu was wrong.

When Ivan and Olaf arrived at the lake, they immediately set to work stacking giant ice blocks. Much to everyone's surprise, Ivan and Olaf had entered the Fabulous Ice Sculpture Contest *together*. All through the day they chipped, sawed, and carved at the ice—without a single argument!

A huge crowd gathered when the judges arrived late in the afternoon. The people followed while the judges carefully inspected every frozen creation.

Finally, they came to the very last entry. Ivan and Olaf stood by their sculpture watching the judges nervously. The crowd fell silent as they looked up at the towering piece of ice.

Staring back down at the crowd was a glorious, gigantic fish. His scales shimmered in the sunlight. His fierce eyes twinkled, and his mouth was frozen in the slightest of smiles.

METHUSELAH
by
Ivan & Olaf
"Best Friends"

CARN

The crowd went wild when the judges presented
Ivan and Olaf with the trophy for first place.
The men posed with their trophy by
the base of the sculpture, where
they had carved these
words:

METHUSELAH
by
Ivan & Olaf
"Best Friends"